A Monkey Ate My Homework

Matt Price

BEACON HILL PRESS
OF KANSAS CITY

Copyright 2007
by Beacon Hill Press of Kansas City

Printed in the United States of America

ISBN-10: 0-8341-2287-1
ISBN-13: 978-0-8341-2287-1

Cover Design: Darlene Filley
Illustrator: Paula J. Becker

Editor: Donna Manning
Assistant Editor: Allison Southerland

Note: This fictional story about three third-culture kids is set in authentic Cotonou, Benin in Africa. It is part of the *Kidz Passport to Missions* curriculum.

10 9 8 7 6 5 4 3 2 1

DEDICATION

To third-culture kids, those who grow up in a culture different from the one where they were born.

CONTENTS

1
Batter Up!

"Drop the bat!" yelled Mr. Reynolds.

"What?" called Shin, as he hurried toward first base with the bat still in his hand.

"Drop the bat before you run to first base," instructed Mr. Reynolds. "Otherwise, someone could get hurt."

Mr. Reynolds was a Nazarene missionary in Cotonou [coh-tuh-NEW], Benin [buh-NEEN] in Africa. He often volunteered to teach the students at the British school how to play American softball. His wife, Mrs. Reynolds, was a teacher at the school. They both knew many of the students and were a Christian influence in their lives.

Shin tossed the bat aside and stood on first base, wondering what to do next. He had watched a couple of South Korean baseball games when he was home during school break. But this was the first time he had played "softball."

"OK, who's the next batter?" asked Mr. Reynolds.

"Me!" yelled Rishi [REE-shee].

"All right, Rishi. Batter up! Remember to stand with your feet apart and your elbow up. And keep your 'eyes on the ball.'"

"'Eyes on the ball?' That sounds weird," thought Rishi Kapoor, whose home country was India.

Whoosh! Rishi swung hard and missed the ball.

"That's OK," encouraged Mr. Reynolds, as he pitched the second ball low and straight.

Rishi saw it coming. *PING!* The ball dribbled toward third base.

"Nice hit! Now, run!" yelled Mr. Reynolds. "Shin, you run too. Go, go, go!"

Rishi ran to first base, then on toward second. Shin almost ran into the kid catching the ball at second base. Shin spun around and landed on his belly on top of the base.

"Rishi, get back to first base!" shouted Mr. Reynolds, waving his arms wildly.

Rishi turned and sprinted toward first base, while the second base player threw the ball

long and high. The first base player leapt high, but the ball flew over his head.

"Now run to second base, Rishi!" yelled Mr. Reynolds.

"This game doesn't make sense at all," thought Rishi.

As Shin brushed the dust from his pants, he saw Rishi running toward him.

"Shin, Mr. Reynolds says you can go to third base," called Rishi, still trying to figure out on what planet this game was invented.

"Third base, here I come!" exclaimed Shin.

"OK, maybe we've played enough softball today," sighed Mr. Reynolds. "Let's play soccer, I mean, football."

"Wait, Mr. Reynolds!" exclaimed Frances. "Don't I get a turn?"

Frances Kpodo walked to the plate like she knew what she was doing. In fact, she did. Her African-American mother was an all-star softball player in college. She taught Frances a lot about softball. Her father, who was from Benin, taught her how to play soccer.

Frances stood at the plate, feet apart and elbow up, waiting for Mr. Reynolds's pitch. *CRACK!* Her bat connected with the ball, and it sailed over the heads of the infielders and the outfielders.

"Run, Rishi! Go, Shin!" yelled Mr. Reynolds, grinning from ear to ear. "Great hit, Frances! That's what we call a 'home run!'"

2
The Assignment

"Class, that's all for today. Don't forget your homework assignment. The one-page paper telling about your most prized possession is due tomorrow. I'll see you in the morning," said Mrs. Reynolds.

Shin, Rishi, and Frances walked through the front gate of the school. The guard smiled

and waved good-bye. Cars and their drivers were waiting to pick up students who were leaving the school.

"Bye," Frances called to the boys as she slid open the side door of the black SUV.

"Hey, Shin," said Rishi, "do you want to come over to my house and do some home-work before dinner?"

"I'm not sure I'll have time," said Shin. "My mother wants me to buy some fruit on the way home. I need to catch a ride on a motorcycle taxi. I'll call you later on my cell phone."

"OK. I'll talk to you then," said Rishi, as he got into the car with his father.

Shin tightened the straps of his backpack and waved his arm at a passing motorcycle taxi.

The driver of the zimmijahn [ZIM-mee-jahn] wore a bright yellow shirt. He sped past Shin, then made a half-circle turn and stopped in front of him.

"I want to go to the market. How much will it cost?" asked Shin.

"Six hundred francs (one U.S. dollar and 20 cents)," the taxi driver answered.

"Oh, no, no, no," said Shin, smiling and

shaking his finger back and forth. "That's too much."

The taxi driver shrugged his shoulders.

"I could pay 250 francs (50 U.S. cents)," offered Shin.

Now it was the taxi driver's turn to smile and shake his finger. "No, that's not enough. It will cost 400 francs (80 U.S. cents)."

Shin smiled. "I can give you 300 francs (60 U.S. cents)."

"That's good enough," said the taxi driver. He motioned for Shin to get on the zimmijahn.

Shin put on his helmet and climbed on the motorcycle behind the driver. He grabbed the bar around the seat's edge to make sure he stayed on the zimmi. The driver looked up and down the street and then sped away.

Shin felt the wind on his arms. He bounced with the bumps in the road. The driver weaved left and right through the cars, bicycles, and other motorcycle taxis. Shin smiled. If only his friends in South Korea could see him now!

3

ZIPPING AROUND ON A ZIMMI

"Stop here," called Shin, pointing toward one of the fruit stands along the roadside.

The driver stopped the taxi in front of a woman who was selling fruit.

"Good day, Mama," Shin said. In Cotonou, Shin had learned to call any woman old enough to be his mother by the title, "Mama."

"What would you like today? Pineapples, oranges, or bananas?" asked the woman.

Shin looked at the fruit stacked in piles shaped like pyramids. "I think my mother wants some pineapples and bananas," said Shin.

"Would you like the long green bananas or the short yellow ones?"

"The short yellow ones," answered Shin. "Those are my favorite."

"Here are 4 pineapples and 10 bananas." The woman handed Shin two plastic sacks. "I included two mangoes for your mother." She smiled. "I know your mother likes my fruit the best."

"How much will the fruit cost?" asked Shin.

"Seven hundred francs (one U.S. dollar and 80 cents)," said the woman.

"Here's one 500 franc coin and two 100 franc coins. Thanks," Shin said. "Have a good evening."

The woman smiled and waved good-bye.

"Over here!" yelled Shin, waving to a passing zimmijahn.

The taxi driver, wearing a dusty NASCAR cap with his yellow shirt, pulled up beside Shin. After some discussion, the driver accepted what Shin offered to pay him.

"Are you ready?" asked the driver.

"I'm ready," replied Shin. He balanced one sack on each knee, while carrying his backpack on his shoulders. Somehow, he stayed on the back of the zimmi as it pulled into the busy traffic.

When the back tire slid off the road, sand and stones flew into the air. The driver's zimmijahn almost bumped into two young men walking with boxes balanced on their heads. When the driver pulled the zimmi back on the road, he weaved around a bicycle and two children walking home from school. He turned left and then right between a car and a dump truck.

"Go left at the phone booth," directed Shin. "Then turn right after the newspaper stand."

The driver turned from a paved street onto the dirt road where Shin lived. As the zimmi bumped and bounced down the road, the driver swerved to avoid a large pothole filled with broken pieces of concrete. Shin pointed down the street toward his house. The zimmi sent chickens running in every direction as it neared Shin's home.

When they stopped, Shin paid the driver 250 francs and thanked him.

The driver nodded at Shin and bounced down the dirt road looking for another customer.

Shin coughed from the dust and exhaust in the air; but underneath his helmet, he was smiling.

4

THE CHOKBO

"Good day, Martin," said Shin to the guard who was sitting at the front gate of his house.

"Hello, my boy. How was school today?" asked Martin.

"It was very good. Thank you for asking."

"Let me take those sacks for you," insisted Martin.

As they walked through the metal gate, they ducked under pink flowers with thorny branches growing on the wall that surrounded the house. Before Shin could find the key in his backpack, a heavy wooden door opened.

"Welcome home," said Clementine, the woman employed to help cook and clean the house. "It looks like you brought something delicious for us to eat. Martin, I'll take those sacks into the kitchen."

Shin could tell Clementine was preparing kalbi [KAHL-bee]. He loved the nutty smell of Korean pork ribs and sesame seed sauce.

"Shin, your mother is in the study," Clementine called from the kitchen.

"Thanks, Madame Clementine." Shin removed his backpack and joined his mother in the study.

The walls of their study were lined with shelves of books. Some books were written in Korean and French, but most were written in English.

"Hello, Mother. How are you doing?" asked Shin politely in Korean.

"Good afternoon, Son. I'm glad to see you. Did you get the fruit for dessert tonight?"

"Yes, Mother. The Mama at the fruit stand even gave us two mangoes," said Shin, grinning at the thought of the sweet, juicy fruit.

"Oh, that's very good!"

"What are you doing?" asked Shin, sitting down beside his mother at the computer.

"I'm looking at some pictures of me when I was slightly older than you. Your grandmother scanned the old photos into the computer and E-mailed them to me." She pointed at the digital photograph on the screen and smiled.

"You look pretty in that dress, Mother."

"Thank you," she replied. "It was my fa-

vorite dress. I had no idea my mother still had a photo of me wearing it."

"I'm not sure what my favorite possession is," said Shin. "I like my video games, but my friends have the same ones. How can a thing be my most prized possession when someone else has the same thing?"

"I've been waiting to give something to you. I think now is a good time." His mother reached up and pulled from the shelf a large book with a brown cover. "This is our family's Chokbo [CHOK-boh]. It's a record of our family members dating back 200 years. The books are not as popular today as they used to be. But your father and I want you to know about your family's history. So we decided to gather information into this book. As the oldest son in our family, the Chokbo belongs to you. Your family is one of the greatest gifts you possess."

"Wow!" exclaimed Shin. "I know what I'm going to write about for my homework assignment tomorrow."

5

A Biscuit and a Backpack

BEEP! BEEP! BEEP! Shin's alarm signaled it was time to get up.

"Is it morning already?" groaned Shin. His glow-in-the dark clock showed 6:30 A.M.

Within an hour, Shin was in front of his house, waiting for a zimmijahn. He was going to Rishi's house. They were going to meet Frances at the bakery and buy some cookies, or biscuits as they call them in Cotonou. Then they were going to walk together to school. A zimmijahn soon pulled up, and Shin headed to Rishi's house.

Rishi was waiting for Shin at his front gate. The two boys walked together and talked about school.

"Did you finish your assignment for Mrs. Reynolds?" asked Shin.

"Yes. It didn't take long for me to choose my favorite possession. I chose my new David

Beckham Real Madrid jersey. David is my favorite footballer. I told how my father bought the jersey while he was on a trip to England last year. Did you finish your homework?"

"Yes, I finished my paper late last night. It tells about my family's history. The record of our history is called a Chokbo. My paper is right here in my backpack."

"There's Frances," said Rishi. "Her car just pulled up to the bakery. Let's go."

Rishi and Shin watched until there were no trucks, cars, zimmis, or bicycles in their path, and then they darted across the street.

"Good day!" Frances greeted Shin and Rishi. The three friends zigzagged through the people going into and out of the popular bakery. A few minutes later, they were walking to school, licking chocolate off their fingertips.

"Look over there," said Frances. "There's a monkey."

"Where's a monkey?" Rishi looked up in the tree.

"It's in front of that large house," Frances said, pointing toward a red cage.

"I wonder why it's sitting outside in a cage," said Rishi.

"Maybe it's someone's pet," said Frances.

"Let's go look at it," suggested Shin. "We have time before school starts."

"OK," agreed Frances.

"Oh, I don't think that's a good idea," warned Rishi. "I've read about monkeys. They can be dangerous."

"It's in a cage," Shin said.

"We'll just look at it," added Frances, as they moved cautiously toward the cage.

"Be careful!" Rishi stayed several steps behind them.

"I will," whispered Shin, as he leaned toward the monkey. "Hey, monkey, do you want some breakfast? Here's a biscuit. It's real good."

Shin held out his open hand toward the monkey. Frances watched over his shoulder, while Rishi kept his distance.

"Whoa! What are you doing?" yelled Shin.

The monkey grabbed the biscuit with one fist, and in a split second, grabbed the strap of Shin's backpack with the other.

Rishi shouted, "He's trying to get your backpack! Quick! Get away!"

Frances and Rishi started running. Shin

twisted one way and then another. Finally, he broke loose. As he ran, his backpack fell to the ground. He quickly snatched it up and kept running.

"Are you OK?" gasped Frances. "You could have been hurt!"

"Uh-oh," said Rishi, pointing back at the monkey. "I think he took something out of your backpack."

"Oh, no!" exclaimed Shin. "It's my home-work paper!"

As the monkey popped the biscuit into his mouth, he showed his sharp teeth and made a giggling sound. Then he tore the paper in two pieces and started chewing it. After a few seconds, the monkey screamed in disgust and spit out the paper chunks.

"My homework!" Shin whimpered. "A monkey just ate my homework."

Prized Possessions

"Good morning, class," said Mrs. Reynolds. "I hope everyone completed their homework assignment. You may tell us about your most prized possessions after sports class. Today, you're going to play softball with Mr. Reynolds."

"Ugh!" cried all those who liked football (soccer) better than American softball. Shin, Frances, and Rishi were trying to catch their breath from their run-in with the monkey.

Mrs. Reynolds continued, "Before you leave, turn in your assignments." The students filed past her desk, leaving their papers.

"Thank you, Frances. Very good, Rishi," encouraged Mrs. Reynolds. "Shin, could you stay behind for a few moments?"

The rest of the students went to their sports class. Shin stood at Mrs. Reynolds's desk, looking down at his feet.

"Shin, I noticed you didn't turn in your assignment. You always turn in your work."

"Well, I, I," stammered Shin.

"What happened?" asked Mrs. Reynolds.

"Well," began Shin, "I did do my homework. In fact, I was up late last night finishing it. My paper was about my Chokbo, a book about my family's history. Since I'm the oldest son in my family, I inherit the responsibility to work on it."

"That sounds very interesting, Shin. But you haven't told me what happened to your homework," said Mrs. Reynolds, with a slight smile.

"Yes, well," Shin continued, "a monkey ate my homework on the way to school today."

"What ate your homework?" Mrs. Reynolds was trying very hard not to laugh.

"A monkey ate my homework," repeated Shin. "I saw the monkey chewing on my paper. Then he spit it out."

"I believe you," Mrs. Reynolds said. "Although I have to admit, I've never heard a better excuse."

"I'm disappointed in myself," said Shin. "I really wanted to do well on this assignment. My family is important to me. It was difficult for my mother to leave South Korea. And it's difficult to live so far from our family."

"I understand," said Mrs. Reynolds. "It was exciting, yet difficult for Mr. Reynolds and me to move here with our two children. We knew our children would be third-culture kids. They might feel like strangers in the country where they were born, as well as the country where they live."

"Do you have family here in Benin?" asked Shin.

"No. We miss our family a lot. It helps us to know we are part of a Christian family who lives around the world and believes in Jesus Christ."

"We attended a Christian church in South Korea," said Shin.

"A Christian family is important too," explained Mrs. Reynolds. "Christians encourage, support, and pray for one another. That's one way we show God's love and set an example for others. God's Word says, 'How great is the love the Father has lavished on us, that we should be called children of God! And that is what we are' (1 John 3:1). God even calls us His 'treasured possession' (Exodus 19:5)."

"I would like to know more about the Christian family. I think my mother would too.

She might not be so lonely if she met other Christians."

"Frances comes with her family to our Bible study every week," said Mrs. Reynolds. "Ask her for directions if you and your family would like to join us."

"Thanks, Mrs. Reynolds."

"You're welcome, Shin. Now, go play softball. Mr. Reynolds is organizing another team. You can turn in your assignment tomorrow. Just stay away from that monkey!"